ABOUT

STEPHEN JAMES PITTERS' poems have a specific nuance, yet they take the calculated risks of exposing his innermost thoughts. His spontaneity employs the conscious and the unconscious as he works his way through the past in varying degrees of reflection. He uses sentiment without being sentimental.

Honest expressions and unbridled emotions provide the reader with a sense of intimacy and invites them into his and the America's histories where interracial relationships were often salted with violence, imprisonment, and even death.

He writes in the people's words without reliance on corporate and academic styles or formulaic conventions so pervasive in contemporary poetry. He uses the politics of emotions. How lovers plot to embrace or to escape their entanglements.

Stephen holds Masters' degrees in Clinical Social Work from Simmons School of Social Work, Boston MA.and University of Pittsburgh School of Public Health as well as a Bachelor of Arts degree from Centenary College in Shreveport, LA. and a Teaching Certificate from Gonzaga University in Spokane, WA. And has hosted The Spokane Open Poetry Program on KYRS Thin Air Community Radio since 2004.

He currently produces Poetry Rising at many different Spokane libraries.and has provided poetry, prose, and music events for senior centers in the area of Spokane.

Stephen also does poetry readings for the local libraries in his area and at local high schools. He's done poetry presentations in Idaho, Washington, and at local high Schools: Gonzaga Prep, North Central, Stevens County: and at Spark Central. He is negotiating family genealogy presentations as well.

Consequence of
LIVING

Consequence of
LIVING

STEPHEN JAMES PITTERS

Dedication:
To the SCENIC boat river CREW while on the
Danube. To some I gave the name "Constellation
Hardis Major" for their hard three weeks of splendid
work. I wish them well for
their lives ahead.

About the book:
The focus is on the experiences afforded to me by so many individuals this year both in the US and the travelers encountered on trips abroad in Western and Eastern Europe. Life the world over holds many similarities, such as hard-working individuals and families attempting to improve their daily lives.

CONTENTS

Contents

THE JUNGLE

Life is a jungle filled with many hazards.
My feelings were teeming,
teeming through my belly,
up and down the spine.

The hacking had me packing.
From these desires I must not sully myself,
but choose to award the expedition by gently packing
instead of throwing this disturbed body onto the floor.

I plead for more a decade ago.
Back then she was all there is
that seemed valuable.

The sultry queen knew what she wanted
and took it with groping hands
 and hard forceful pressing lips.
Desire was her squire who hunted slily.

She pranced from noon to dusk
And in so doing garnered my trust very easily.
I was in over my head, however.
Though often I thought, I must be in heaven.
The fact was, I had entered the gates of hell
accompanied under her spell.

I long suspected and detected.
She was a mad trance
looking for any hot romance
and gave it whatever acts
would yield her favored results.

Lilly fanned my fire until it became a blaze
fully out of control.
My mind found its privilege in a haze.
The daze wrapped itself like a roundabout
in the dreams that followed.

In between minutes I drifted.
Contented not to deny shame
its position as herald to my throne.

Tired of the minor distraction, she halted
the quid-pro-quo, we engaged in.
I felt myself in the instant a crazed wild animal
lacking sustenance.

Unable to free myself, the only thought that prevailed
was "if you don't go for more, it will be gone from this jungle
without any further hope of seeding this life".

WHEN I LOOKED AT HER

When I looked at her
My world lost its gloominess.
Her soft ocean blue eyes
cast a net over my dumbstruck heart.

I felt torn apart
Though I didn't bleed.
I sped up and was conceived
like a child exiting the womb.

The joy locked in hope was released.
I shrieked internally, like a once lonely wolf
who had found an engagement,
with his new soul mate.

Fate stood before me and revealed
my long-awaited miraculous salvation.

Out of the blue what was due had come through.
The fragrance of honey wafted between our inches
and mad oscillating vibrations.

Being removed these many years from exultation,
terminated its ploy.
I was no longer absent from blissful exhilaration.
Her soft creamy allure had opened the door
to a vaunted universe.

To know this rapturous experience
brought my reality to its knees.

Misery's disease was put at ease.
My heart at last was pleased.

AS LONG

As, long as, I live.
As, long as, I strive.
As, long as, one good day goes by,
and I try to be decent and respectful,
to another person's life.

I will have fulfilled the reason
for which I was originally
placed on this earth.

To judge another's worth
is to decrease their value
and assault their dignity.

It is not the wish.
It is what you accomplish with it.

MARK THE COURSE

Footprints coming and going
mark themselves in the snow.
Blood highlighted their trail.

The stories they told,
where that of men and women
being very bold attempting to survive
the cold crossing the plains.

Their aim is to reach
the shores along the great Pacific Ocean.
The trek asked much of them.
The determined saw the wonder.

The meek squandered themselves
before ever seeing
the Rockies or the Great Salt Lake.

They carried hope when leaving Saint Louis
but the harsh terrain and bandits
gobbled it in Kansas.

Nature's wrath was the war,
these Pilgrims were ill prepared to battle.
Brotherhood and friendship
held most of the inquisitive travelers together
but their faith would be tested
when ice pellet storms whipped them severely.

Some cried while others died inside,
for other pioneers to find
 the following spring or summer.
Bleached bones and wooden crosses
marked their epitaph.

Cruelty is the profound harbinger
for dreams attempting to risk one's life
based on possibilities.

What had to be done
lay in the heart of the spirit
that carried the Good Lord in it.

Over the span of time, they continued
and finally reached fertile lands,
rich in green grass and cool clean waters.

Natural homes were built with great enthusiasm.
Cattle empires and wild mustang horses
also contributed to their wealth and ingenuity.

The cost however was the loss
to those who were there for centuries before
living in harmony with nature
but couldn't stay ahead of the new barbarians
who brought with them
disrespect, dishonor, and lewd firepower.

Their end however continues to this day
in a very sad way on the age old rocky, stark, reservation.

CARING

It is the little things, a kind word, a show of concern,
a warm smile, the touch on your arm, a common gift
like a chocolate square that heals the heart
when life is facing a dire ordeal.

Those quiet emotional offerings
gives us pause to reflect and find hope again.
They ask us to renounce the hopelessness
which strangles our sense of purpose.

We are called to resurrect the beauty still in life
and treasure the past we had
and the future we know awaits.

These hopes are priceless in the face of fear.
They patrol the avenues where the spirit sings
and life begins and ends.
They light the stage for the second coming.
We hoped to see.
Letting doubt remain a tardy bystander,
unlike fulfillment which is, the cheerful scholar
who labored for the destiny on the horizon.
Before the stars in the heavens felt the need to depart.

THE BLOW

A brief flow of common sense
loaned us its altruism.
I came in her smile
which rescued us
from a great discomforting divide.

Wisdom has a way of finding
the right path on which to travel
when turbulence rages,
confusing which direction should be taken.

A deep breath, a warm bath, a pleasing violin sonata
can each serve to displace indignation
from taking the lead with furious speed.

Off times we are quick to seek an exit
when need is not met satisfactorily,
but followed by sorrow and regret.
The choking fumes then rise and rise.
The gray darkness catapults itself into every phase
of awareness and cries multiplies.
War begins to trip us over each other.
Hurt and harm plows through the consciousness.
Distress has little to confess
after disrespect wields its justification.

Loss managed to continue floundering.
Its olive branch snatched from the fingers
that scraped the skin.
Pins and needles would not cease punishing
the alleyways of the mind.

Life it appears never thought it would be left behind.
Wading in the gutter compiling gunk however
had twisted the soul,
leaving only foul humors to unravel
the decrepitude listed in our closing days.

BETTER IS FOREVER

I, reached and stretched across time.
The physical space stood solid harnessing my emotions
that I may see and feel the intense love
I had inside me for this animal's existence.

He was and is the best of my lifetime experiences.
The most considerate, thoughtful, and supportive,
when emotional cruelties descended through me
leaving my spirit nearly crushed.

Wondering in the lanes, of those psychic occurrences,
I neared the edge of self-sacrifice.
His fruitful appearance served to solidify the voice of hope
which conquered the hammer of doubt
and calmed anger's confusion.

Let it not be said or thought
that this once mortal creature failed
but was man's absolute iron post.
Diesel as was Arny, the imperial, majestic force
that surrounded my occasional, wavering,
 psychological constitution closing the gap
that impeaches.

Love is and will forever be the bridge
between us
that lingers without apprehension.

———⦿———

MAGIC'S CHARM

The acid drops, carves a circular hole into the pliant shield,
delivering heat to the heart of the steel,
making this alloy of iron and carbon
cry out loud when gored.

We achieved throes
during the pleasing altercation
of the wonderful titillations,
traveling through our lucid expectations
without any doubt,
accepting only the creeping designs
which coated our bodies through the night.

When good had ended, we begged for more,
permitting relief to believe
that tomorrow would not be the thief
attempting to be brief.

Our hopes pursued its course nevertheless
knowing the magic could not rest
after its previously surmounted test.

The voodoo queen not withstanding
had rolled, cast forth the bones.
Giving us the means of the loud sound deposited
from the golden trombone.
Oh my! oh my! "life, chose not to die", they said.

ANTI- CONVERSATIONS

Some fill the room with themselves.
Their echo reverberates off the ceiling and walls.
The more they talk, the more they inflate
and irritate the skin of the Good Samaritan
who must tolerate the sounds of these frenzied vibrations.

Civility under these circumstances
is put into an odious, repulsive, coercive state.
The mind is embattled,
a slow feeling of anger swells.

The thought of escaping begins to chart its course.
Once such emotions were pleasant anticipations.
Rust, now has gathered and the value of the trip
has begun to sink to the bottom of the drink.

The taste of being in this company is foul.
Discussions between the participants are reactive.
Thoughts are not easily extended but cut short.
A defensive posture grows in one's heart.
The gnarling has come calling.

The bridge rises and forms a pyramid in this desert
like an approaching whirling crisis
ever since "the all-knowing"
circumvents each direction offered.

The attitude proffered is self-serving,
that of self-importance which overlooks all else
like facts listed in the Encyclopedia Britannica.

It speaks to being above others like self-righteousness
or the blowfish which takes up every inch of the dish
but, the quality, is mediocre.

Each day the tension grew greater
and the rubble caused more trouble,
in their environment.

Contradictions continued to shout like a flame
that burns more severely.

Living in this field of play
shouted, "foul" to no one's dismay.
Each finally went their own way.

THE SQUEEZE

While moving about, through numerous landscapes,
that were the homes to mountains, valleys,
and country sides,
I advanced into a few placid botanical floral gardens.

The varies there, housed purple gardenias, tulips,
yellow roses, and bronze philodendrons.
Each were advancing through different levels of maturation.

Their developments displayed certain energies.
Some issued a smooth cautious warmth.
Others demonstrated their intense dynamic hellos
whose show was openly receptive to anything new.

The captivating qualities of these individual flowers
attracted my means to exit
and enjoy the days that passed before me.
I seldom hesitated to continue any flavorful, tasty discussion.

Whenever I stood near one these rows
 I felt their sensations driving me forward
and chose to entertain them as a reward
or a gift offered by life
to anyone who is willing to risk
living a little more for the time given him
and knew he must not squander the opportunity

that may never return,
but suddenly, mercilessly taken away,
by a random display,
of callous detachment.

LOOKING INSIDE

To love more requires empathy's offering
which renounces openly any immediate judgments
but instead, is disposed to truthfully accept
differences that abound outside one's own
narrow, immediate parameters of understanding.

Feeling free to give oneself without misgivings,
without question, provides a new ceiling
whose view is extended, reachable
when the mind, body, and spirit
relinquishes fear, and summary rejection.

What had previously resided, buried within
 the narrow confines of philosophical obstruction
was removed by the will to do so.

The capability to explore new worlds, trends,
and hopes, using strong beliefs to explore dimensions
of time and space
allows for resolutions that catapults the possible
without the need for the old guardians to be maintained
and the self-inclined, prepared to welcome the unknown.

For such is love,
 a visit to the great beyond,
to a place far, yet near,
and sometimes very eager, very eager, to stay.

LEAVING THE FUTURE

The falling leaves of time
swished over the rough ground.
They buried the weak from the strong
that couldn't manage to hold on.

The loss of face was not seen
when death's charm hung in between
the hollows of the spleen.

The call went out
to the jaws of sadness.
It didn't respond immediately
but lingered on and on, fretting.

On the cool moist ground,
the arms of the few cuddled
and muddled around, lost in the belly
of what was seemingly profound.

On themselves, they painted
the look of withered consternation.
Harm had healed in them
the mark of the penitent.

Again, the call went out.
Its shout wondered about
in a quizzical daze,

whose crazed deliberations
mocked their praise worthiness.

How would they live or function
when direction and cause
knew only the means to their extinction?

The fire they started marched forward
with one hardened industry,
the black earth policy.

In the final turn, the weary methods
of their extremes blew them away
like a grey puff of smoke
climbing into the dark, cloudy,
worn through heavens.

NOW BEFORE THEN

What has been done is done.
What we choose to do now
is the link to the future
that is yet to be determined
or concluded.

We once had something
we valued and sought to perpetuate.
This became known as fact
but fiction altered its perpetuity.

We searched our minds
and inspired possibilities
which we crafted as the foundations,
the bedrock to an alternate reality.

We continued our search,
bursting and building,
restoring new substances.

Our beliefs took hold.
Bold excavations unearthed
miracles which seeped through,
which led to a new canvas
that celebrated colors upon colors called the rainbow.

We were bestowed a highway into the present.
It relinquished the past.
A new set of documents where organized.

They formed a bible, a philosophy,
a non-conforming neutrality, called science
which was to be the challenge
that enlists perpetuity.

Now will, with its will,
act as guiding principles which instills hope,
to always continue where love presents
to its members the choice they always have
to proceed and intercede
rather than plaintively accept
and be diminished.

Tomorrow will arrive,
only if today, now thrives.

We can only be the host,
participants in the universe
if we continue to accept the challenges
that face us day by day,
and pray they never go away.

We are here to overcome,
what must to be done!

By attacking the hill,
we get to arrive and view a glimpse,
ford the minutes we are to inherit.

CREATION

An idea that hurled itself
into my mind,
became a story, I need not,
could not, leave behind.

There was intension
to the design of the purpose.
I had little need to strain my brain
for it to take a deep hold.

When such an august breeze,
desires its feed,
it will feel like home.

The heart thereafter will rise to know,
forgiveness and compassion,
are the true configurations
immaculate love inhabits.

Love, for those who found it,
 know one thing which is,
it lives within, triumphant,
never at a loss to supply… satisfaction.

THE HEART'S VOICE SPOKE

If you could feel what I see,
the world would pause its tears.

My voice rose within
when your smile crossed over to me,
without having to hide.

Our harmony railed,
unable to stand still.

My roaring will did not presume
but chose to consume your nature,
before nighttime could sprinkle its magic
against the starry heavens.

I ask again,
can you see what I feel?
If so, then trust your instincts,
they are the motivators
of joy's unaltered rest.

Try, then try, and try once more
to understand, how grand you are, life has just blessed me.
I see now, the daily rhythms that conspired
to afford me another opportunity at survival.
When you came, blame was tamed.

You heard and saw what I felt
and let your slow, quiet, determined love
deal me the winning hand.

SUPERFICIAL

The fight was on.
I tried hanging strong.
In the first few rounds, her animal magnetism dug in,
like a right cross smashing against the chin.

She moved about remaining outside of calm.
Her pulse began to beat rapidly.
Her breath ushered some beaded steam.
Her eyes rolled over backward, like a demon white shark
about to snap its jaws into its prey's sorry flesh.

She reached the point of addressing her enticement.
Between us there was no further separation
only the consummation of a heated desire
that had waited its turn, its yearning from long ago.

We persisted with the fruitful exploration,
exhorting what we knew was required
in order, to celebrate living harder
like die hard mountaineers roaming free
in the wilderness of their imagination before it evaporated.

Arriving at the pinnacle of our dreams,
the haze between us had thickened.

Two fools who were once amused
are now, instead bemused by their effort gone wrong,

and their foolish weakness,
that found its shadow folded at sundown.

To recover and face the sun,
demanded the ultimate sacrifice.

The battle to achieve this glory didn't press on.
The clang of the baleful bells rang out
with only a pitiful clout,
that announced the end of their dulling bout
which was a superficially collapsed relationship
still in mourning.

CONSEQUENCE OF LIVING

"A woman can be polite," mocked the chocolate haired,
sparkling green eyed, blue jeaned mare,
opening the door before me.

Swishing her willowy figure, as she approached the knob,
stirred my energies abruptly.
The stallion in me readied itself to respond.

I thought, will her motivation last beyond the few seconds,
 that we crossed each other's earthly path?
Will she think about me for a while thereafter
or was this bravado, retailing her allure?

In the alley of my chambered heart,
 I wished for more displays of her forceful nature.
She had scored a high soaring trey from deep
that swept me off the floor.

Possibility dangled through our eyes
with the eagerness it comprised.
Which of us knew, wanted, or would leave the door
to our feelings and emotions ajar?

I was being introduced to a woman,
one with confidence, knowledge,
and the experience of social activities.

She was aware of a certain level of comfort
and its offerings when she traveled the streets
both day and night.

In our face-to-face instant, she forwarded them to me.

She knew and felt within, what could be,
if she chose to confer upon herself
the tasteful effect of a myriad of innuendos.

I kept feeling myself being drawn into her rush.
The closer we circled though briefly.
The communion grew more easily.

Four strides and three yards apart,
we passed through the mercantile door.
The birds each went separately
to their own destinations.
The chirping finished.

Nature doesn't frown over what it conducts.
It merely proceeds again selecting what it must transact.
Going my way and she hers, I was glad to have
remotely conspired in the emotional touch
that had instantly satisfied the short collusion.

My hope nevertheless is that afterwards,
She or another of equal grace
would perhaps enter my wondering eyes.

The consequence of living is being or
sometimes coming close
without obtaining a heavy enough dose.

The cigar didn't really get lit.
It only slipped. ++++++++++++++

TERROR'S PRESENCE

Fire doth eat
at all along the avenues
where it creeps.
Sorrow measured the depths of its deceit.

Rows upon rows, the prickly heat swept aside.
The valued flowery treats unable to run and hide.
Helpless and charred,
they were formed into mounds of blackened ash.

These petal fellows hollered loudly at the crowds
that traveled miles to view their majesty,
before the evil heat
grabbed and uprooted their feet.
The jolt cost them the splendor they once had.

Their cries failed to subsist.
The punishment seemed
a harrowing maltreatment
to plants who only staged beauty
we couldn't resist.

The swiftness of mother nature's wrath
had surprised the poor, panicked citizens
who were at a loss
to contest her ferocious, fiery, fury.

In a flash, the devastation to their lives, occurred.
The turn of events, came, saw, and conquered
what had been sewn over years,
lending joy to many hearts, minds, and emotions.

A darkened perplexing question remained
like a stain wherever their terrain stretched.
Across a broad distance, shelters lay tattered.
Perceived only as a sad memory,
but once conceived, a glowing dream.

A dream however,
that in the shock of the moment,
"a good sun should not be afraid
to rise and set upon, once more."

SEEING THE UNSEEN, YET

"It is not impossible
only yet to be done",
spoke the mind to the spirit, eyes,
fingers, hands, feet, legs, and back.

Ask the heart to pump harder.
Call the imagination, it may be journeying
somewhere north
where blue- silver stars trex.

When all is defused,
what is terrible,
is also removed.

Reason and logic, knows its value.
They, are able, to overcome conflicts
that crowd the necessary path traveled.

Peace will then follow
And we as one can enjoy
what the Lord ordained
for us to encompass on this earth.

WILD STORMS

From now till the gates of heaven closes,
my hands dreamt of hosting
your soft, tender, supple body.

I promised never to be late
nor ever desire to escape
its winsome demands.

Her shape is the artist temple,
a stampede of colorful flowers
whose charm serves only to disarm.
Whatever happens is no rolling trifle.

The grappling will ease and please.
Between the minutes and hours of our procession,
we came to know how innocence was lost
and the cost,
which was worth the knowledge, we gained.

Abstaining was not ever preferred.

Our canvas was painted with extreme patience,
and masterful, determination.
"Da Vinci" in his unconsciousness
could have been peering from on high
without wondering why not.

Both our souls were being hung
to rival the view of eternity.

At the beginning we treated each other very well
and where profusely contented.
We dwelled in the aftermath of binding necessity,
before the intensity faded poorly.

Its grip released itself
from the hold of a fabulous engagement.
A modicum of electric charge barely remained in us,
until no further appeal could keep-up the toll.

She was fetching in her prime,
delicious, and pleasing.
Uncontested beyond sublime.

In a splash, she emptied out my mind.
Evacuated herself from my wishes
like a wicked storm
obliterating chunks of my carefree disposition.
The parts of me being torn,
were unable to report for their tour of duty.

The appalling proliferation she applied never ceased.
The beating rose like a screeching greeting.

Madness seemed to have engulfed their castle
like a hurricane breaching its walls,
ripping apart room by room
with a weighted iron broom.

The treasure stores hid
when reached, fell prey to repeated demonic attacks.
Few remains, were necessary to be counted.
What was heard after the crumbling,
was the final explosion of death
strolling over itself.

STOP-OVER

We are just one heartbeat from extinction.
Bonding makes the call to survival,
asking for an extension.

She was the anomaly passing by
 that peaked through,
like a stopover which refreshes the senses,
making fact of the past, present, and future.

The glimpse I had of her deep brown hair,
 magnetic smile, and onyx color eyes
 surprised my direction.

Without knowing, she installed a new hope,
for my purpose to cope more effectively.
Inspiration was urged to deliver an un-obstructed message.
Pure feelings answered with a loud iconic gong.

I trusted its wherewithal to marshal a pleasing impulse,
a divine perspective that will deliver me closer to her spirit.
She was magic and kindness leapfrogging the past,
 intersecting with how future's happiness was designed to
 conjoin.

The dance we could or should explain
had finally been colored brightly
by the meeting that presented itself
unpredictably, rather than with necessity or reason.

Joy is a fluid drink worth imbibing whenever we can.
Our friendly eyes said, "yes to this caring understanding."

A GOOD LIFE

Gracefully extending their artful call
to one and all proved exceptional.
These Roman and Greek-like nymphs
dazzled the attending.

Their flexing motions, spurred intense emotions
that lent itself to sweet commotion.
With stanch will, these dancers' atmospheric insistence
flew themselves through the air
like turtle doves free of despair.

Others like ospreys descended dramatically
intent on gathering the prey,
during the sun's diminishing rays.

The power of their athletic form
pierced the woodwind's profound beats
when the chorus gathered in perfect synchronicity.
Together they provided reassurance
that the story line was on the right path.

The lasting effect revels in its magical transformation.
Their actions palpitate the heart
replete with artistic manifestations
that carries us through the air above
and with emotional flair below.

One by one the company translates
the mystical qualities of past gods and goddesses,
who previously ruled the heavens of old.
The enchantment is their history being told
of love, war, and raging conflicts.

The new modernism expresses
a wide range of forms
that readily disarms one's feelings
with their unique explosions
transported by leaps and bounds.

When the theater doors close
and the lights dim, and the music rises,
what there is of the good life is released within.

THE END NEEDS TO BEGIN

There is an evil wind
crawling over my skin.
It comes whenever the crow squawks
and the acid breeze flows from the mouth of sin.

The litany of plagues rains down
starting with remorseless diatribes,
that hangs me out to dry.
The crucifixion proceeds at a steady pace.

Her lips are transfixed to maim
whatever goal I attempt to attain.
Large or small the wrecking ball
Delivers deadly blow after blow.

Hearing the harsh story she promotes,
punctures my weighted soul.
I work not to be permeated
but the unleashed anger throttles forward
seeking not to dismiss the raw pain
encircling the fishers within my brain.

The oration begins with,
when he travels, he is slow to solve minute items.
He is linear in thought; He says is her answer not his.
He must be interpreted as if I needed to be spoken for.

This array of negativity has persisted year after year.
Each time any crowd gathers, she assumes the right
to lead the discussion at the expense of the attendees.
The light must shine on her head.
Leadership must be hers to wield, regardless of the
circumstance.

Competition is the hat she wears
no matter, the time, place, or venue.

I am not invisible nor destitute.
I was satisfied, not contrite.
I am not out of sorts.
She is not religion to be followed
just a confining, disheartening tempest,
whose fire needs a gigantic dousing
to mire her to the neck in quicksand forever.

The end needs to begin.

FRIENDLINESS CAME FROM OUT OF TOWN

Friendliness has its own
inner, of the heart language.

When affability shows itself,
often through a candid warm smile,
 intense poignant feelings are uplifted
and crosses into the object of its discretion
allowing a certain musical entertainment to follow.

The silent parables spoken or shown,
tranquilizes any fear lurking
that may undermine the sociable presentation.

The pull of the kindly power has a seductive quality
that brings into play a trusting alliance
which generates the need to otherwise pursue.

This benevolent tonic resides in an age-old
heart pounding refinery,
fermenting, improving its fine taste.

Drinking-in, its sympathetic indulgence
has never been a disgrace
only the surprise
which one should never let go, or waste.

The incident of its neighborly allure,
suggested we explore instead

of deplore
or ignore.

Throughout life,
friendliness has served its carrier well
when casting its spell
on the receiver of its aim
in an unanticipated moment,
effortlessly and unknowingly direct.

This good-natured trait justifies the release of an impulse,
which appears to seek a merry contact
that is seldom retracted, mostly enlarged,
energizing for the stranger in its affable walkway
who experiences a similar shocking revelation
and wishes instinctively to accommodate
the growing pleasurable sensation.

The un-staged performance
took a glance at their possibilities
and wondered calmly, is this a dream
or a mirror image of mutual self-esteem?

The pause was a challenge to resume,
 push onward with the clues,
or let mildew and regret accrue,
like a warm winter meaty stew
left to become tastelessly cold?

My mind exploded with seismic, tumultuous hope!

———❧❧❧———

LOOSING THE JOURNEY

Once I knew little of the present
and struggled to determine
what was ordinary or should be.

I accepted fleeting realities,
developing only what I understood
and could easily interpret as fact
rather than fiction.

Time had passed and was now immobile.
My life was crystalized into standing memories
I was sure of and had justified.

Good, bad, or annoying became the citadel
where I lived in comfort
and occasional misrepresentations.

Some of these events were however tarnished
by acrimonious transfusions which didn't fade.
I kept paying for their foreboding presence.
I looked over my shoulders time and again
spending useless vigor
trying to contend with their unwilling capitulation.

The past represented itself staunchly.
Its rule became a stigmatic disaster.
I stretched myself through time
and was able to acquire a better rhyme to install
less I fall into the pit of indecision

which would steal from me
whatever I chose to represent myself.

The present on its arrival,
slowly metamorphized itself
like an uncontaminated, virginal flower.

I bowed, removing past impurities.
Hope brought forth its brush.
I tried administering it.
The effort was not flawless
but it sufficed to render new opportunities
to unburden my spirit.

Time however sped up its agenda.
My body began to wither,
displaying numerous requests for the assistance,
I was unable to promote.

The hour of the sun was setting.
The ticking in the clock became louder.
Disaster flexed its annoyance
through myriads of vested intrigues.

The clashes were with a determined titan.
A villain, who had won every battle he faced.

The pace I positioned had traced the intricacies; I was to
embrace.
I had nothing left
but to tolerate the final loss of the journey.

EVERLASTING COMPANIONS

The morning of the previous fun filled night
accepted my awakening.
She was filled with euphoria
and further thrilling expectancies.

On the carpet, were the sings of gifts scattered
like early Christmas day shouting all around us.
The donations had been intense, jolly contributions
which refused to alter their rotations.

On and on we offered our bounty
without settle-ling for charity
 but dutifully claiming the inheritance granted.

These hours did not try one's soul
 but delivered the entirety of its control
which he was exceedingly willing to transfer.
Pausing had no home nor place for indecision.

Their motors were finely tuned.
They operated together with European precision, flat out,
like on the Autobahn.

Meeting together,
having crossed the winner's line many times,
they held their trophies, very tightly,
rolling and rolling, declaring, crowning themselves
true believers of love's everlasting companion.

⸻⸻ ❧ ⸻⸻

SENSATIONS

55

She showed up again
and I was weakened,
Charmed by her delicious, flagrant solution.

She lit red-hot the brightness
of where I chose to be.

She was again, the dynamic justification
for the proper heart's decision to rejoin
and find for all time its vestibule.

Her passageway is how,
I, through the universe
like mankind finds
his divine participation.

CALLING ON LOVE (CELESTE)

The feeling of a cold, ten-pound iron shotput ball
weighs within the base of my stomach.
It mirrors the pain being inflicted
from the loss of one who could have been
my own flesh and bones.

She, Celeste, was enjoying the best
time had to offer her green years on the planet.
Life for her was sweet.
She filled the hearts of those closest
to her imagination, each day they were exposed
its warmth, charity, love, and devotion.

She started life with pleasant expectations
and spread her joyous nature
like crystal rays
blessing each corner of the earth,
the rest of us called home.

Being close to her was invited love
having the opportunity
to share itself without hesitation.

We felt blessed by her spiritual hugs.
We, her family, did not imagine,
that she would depart,
taken from us this rapidly, this readily.

The heavy cloud is settling,
though hopefully, temporarily,
from each sector of the space
still remaining in our time.

She will never fade from the corners
of our minds and eyes
like a drying blade of grass
but continue to last and last
until our heart's beat, cease.

We cannot be blinded forever however
by the sudden shock of her separation.
Though the light in our spirit had been dulled temporarily,
we sit and mull over the length and breath
in how much her worth expanded our field of living.

The price is never right for such occurrences.
Our faith is that we in time will recover
and fully function again
from the forfeiture of our magnificent jewel
that was plucked, much too early
from her passage through time.

Our minds can never be halted.
It will keep searching, divining the truth
related to how, we can accept the searing blow.

We know overtime will be reduced
as well as the profound hurt attached
alongside this immediate extreme.

The family's deep abiding love nevertheless
serves as a buttress to this seismic wave
which has attempted to wash them
from the safety of the shore.

Love is the main device we have
that can withstand
any unplanned insurrection
to the heart.

SHADY CREATURES

The schooner should have stayed in port
and its crew choose to do something
of greater value rather than raising anchor
and heading towards discovering
a multitude of enticing adventures.

The open seas have always been for some
the call of absolute freedom.
The challenge to test their mettle,
when called upon to do battle
with nature's aggressive behaviors.

Sailors and landlubbers alike
have each reached for the stars, wanting to kiss their beauty
at the earliest opportunity.

In their way have stood
gigantic waves, tornadoes, thunderous squalls
or damaging earthquakes.

The commitment they made to survive
demonstrated their will and bravery
against disturbing odds.

Preparing for these natural oddities
is far beyond anyone's daily reality.
What happens when the consuming forces
present themselves, is the answer character reveals.

We each can enjoy the beautiful golden, purple, orange rays
we see painted on the horizon.
However, the closer we get near to it,
the farther, it still appears to remain afar.

It is a warning that good things must be respected
rather than us attempting to co-op their meaning.

Man is a hunter, forever deeming to acquire
whatever crosses before his dreaming lustful eyes.

Ladies of the world guard your pearls
from carnivorous wayfaring dilettantes
who simply wish to add you to their dusty trophy case.

SEARCHING MY FEELINGS

I needed the sun to wake me up.
For too long I stood in the dark quaking, shaking.
I searched my feelings hoping to discover
The distant love that would steer me above,
above the filth underneath my feet.

I wanted someone to treasure,
One who would say to me, "always and forever
shall we inherit the present and the future".

Throughout the past, I held back, marking time,
wasting my heart and soul.
Mother hope slept while I drifted in desperation
agonizing internally.

Was I the fish entangled in our net
sweating out desire before I died?
I could only whisper please
before the disease called love
allowed me to bleed a bit more
like an experiment
about to be kicked out the door.
A sliver of light finally pushed away the charcoal hazes.

I leaped from the cover when I felt the touch
of her warm friendly breeze penetrating
the hairs above my crown.
Her mouth supplied many answers

that informed me that
never again she would leave this aged soul.
We rolled together, loudly melting into the distant sunset.

When sunrise peaked, we revised the roles
of gratefully happy in a quiet way,
like two hasty turtle doves chirping, chirping at play.
What a day it is to be alive was not questioned.

FULLFILLING PROMISES

Moment after moment would not do.
Moment between moments
had accrued exceptional merit.

We spoke breath by breath
invoking the soul not to be abandoned,
in the wake of undertaking the challenge
living had offered.

Hoping imposed itself at the twelfth hour
requesting that forgiveness intrude
should a slice of selfishness
attempt to misrepresent core principles.

Through the days first light
we feared lingering together,
caressing summer's bold undertaking
might terrorize and mock our budding apprenticeship.

"Save me dear", said I.
She responded "we both are lost
in our fruitful imagination
and curious inspirations.
Each look that transpired eye to eye
was a prayer, a promise revived
by the test our hearts announced,
petitioning further loving entreaties
to salvage the fruit of life.

The term of their study passed with an A+++.
They stayed together well beyond the lights of
their future's awakening exclamations.

The dark was never seen beyond its acceptable place in time,
crying being disarmed.

RISING AND FALLING

The drops of blood were like rubies
being stolen from the bottom of my heart.
I was hurting, hurting because she chose to depart,
departing to start a new quest on the side of another
whose life she presumes would provide her
with greater satisfaction.
Wealth has a fashionable cost-conscious pedigree.

The crushing sound she provided, "saying goodbye"
remained in my mind like the morning iron bell ringing
its death knells.

Her initial shyness was a rouse
which in the end hung me out to dangle,
like a rotting apple filled with worms.
A fantastic distress leaped all over my upper torso.

She covered her benign antics
with a multitude of apparent kindliness
and feigned concerns.
Each gesture or word of praise
was a shovel digging the hole
for my soul to enter its final domain.

She didn't really need love.
She was a witch, the devil masqueraded as,
like a disease sent to slash immature emotions
with unpunished exemption.

After days upon days of retreats, she was captured
and cast into a pit of fits
by he who said to her,
"You really do not measure up
to my standards of excellence".

Fare play had returned to having its say.
I kept myself-once safely restored,
principally at bay.

CHEWING

My world was without
the heat of satisfaction.
I flourished a minute here and there
until she said, "hello don't despair".
She was mom being supportive.

The beauty she provided
brought the heavens to a standstill.
Nothing which once lived
and cherished their previous memories
could repeat those feelings she displayed.

Revolution received a newfound gratitude
without preconceptions.
Belief was revived.
Spiritual stimulation had no need to cry
and tried instead to fly into the arms of joy.
I was a toddler.

The world turned over
like a wheel spinning
or a child losing its early teeth,
before molars and incisors
obtained their reward for chewing,
enjoying, defeating, the full taste of meat.

When a great deal of time passed,
and the body grew stronger,
compliance with proper nutrition
became an everyday abundance
of accumulated behavior.

KEEPING AWAY THE RAIN

Staying was trying to keep the rain away.
Time and again, we were soaked.
The cold followed.

The chill kicked us to the floor.
We tried to recover but being a bit broken
establishes the painful truths
 we were unable to elude.

"Excuse me", she said.
I replied, "that won't do
nor do I care to".

The fall had occurred.
Their fears had come true.
Being unsure is the worse calamity
for two dogs of different breed.

Glaring teeth drips saliva,
 the growling reached into the flesh.
Blood climbed out.
Their dance curled them over
but failed to solve the new direction they took
and instead closed their book.

The show was over in brief fashion.
No further annoyance occurred
between them.

GIVING INTO YOUR WILL

She gave my love a home.
I pushed back harder than intended,
fell through clear down into a shaft
which left no room to regain my regards.

It mattered not.
Commitment held fast to feelings
we presumed had an opportunity to last.

Love knew it was out of control
and kept bearing its needs
with deep passions, flowing over.

Feelings were indisposed
like a wild bull crashing through
the undergrowth uprooting weeds
and other vegetarian lively hoods.

Sanctuary moved aside
whenever we entered time's confinement.
Life was living what it was trained to accomplish,
"Holding fast to the mist and never resisting the beauty
feelings wished to entertain".

One dance with her would do,
to pull us through
and into the caverns where the heavens
would have us remain in peaceful safety.

THE QUEEN'S FLAME
"HOLD STRONG AND CARRY ON"

What can be said
that has not yet been heard
from someone of such magnanimous esteem?
She is and was the Queen of Queens,
the guardian, the guiding star
sitting at the center of their universe
near and far.

Constancy cannot be revoked nor provoke to falter.
In her seven decades as the foundation, the bedrock,
they looked to, for perseverance, she stood firm.
Representing the iron fibers
keeping the Commonwealth solid, unwavering,
when other nations quivered, lost direction,
and sought to destroy their very own constitutions.

Elizabeth II demonstrated the strength of character
from start to finish.
She mirrored the personality known as "A stiff upper lip"
but also revealed a compassionate soul and a caring
disposition for the people within her kingdom.
The Queen loved them and dedicated herself
to serve in their behalf from her twenties'
through adulthood and beyond.

Her life of service to their welfare is without par.
She faced the world's evolving political and social changes,
addressing her own acute personal sorrow,

and painful family losses,
while maintaining her dignity with style and grace.

Joy took their place but could not erase,
blind, tarnish, nor consume her attention to duty.

Sacrifice knew its seat was to be quiet at her table.
She didn't withdraw
nor defer its demands and requirements.
She was steady in love and in service.
Throughout those realities,
she was ever giving in fondness
to her people and her family alike.

Calm and cogent, clear, and devoted.
She maintained herself stoically generation after generation.
Her fire stemmed from selflessness given
rather than selfishness for personal gains
which is often the stain on those who are inherently weak
in character and seek to cheat the office
they are sworn to uphold.

Look not to the west.
They have not displayed their very best.

Royalty is more than a title.
Royalty is deference to enhancing the quality of living,
we were fortunate to have had the opportunity to employ.

Long live the memory of a Queen truly revered.

⸺⧉⸺

OH! CANADA

While on a famous river, the Danube, to which
the world owes a significant debt.
On this sunny autumn day, the representatives
of two friendly nations met.
One from north of the border, the other from south
of the same continent.

An offer of social courtesy was made, in a brotherly gesture.
Do you wish something?
"Tea with honey if you wish", the other stranger replied.
Doubt and humor closing upon his mind.

The two men spoke to each other briefly, courteously,
pleasantly, as though born to be side by side.
Within ten minutes, the hot tea arrived on a tray.
"He had skills", thought the southerner
perhaps learned as a secondary occupation.

"The waiter" drifted away as quickly as he had first
presented himself.
Years between these two cultures
had forged meaningful tides.

Their mutual shores served to bring freedom and survival
for escapees longing to begin anew for centuries.
Miles and miles from the east, south, north, and west,
their hides had suffered under the brutal lash of oppressive
political, religious, and social revisionist activities.

Historically for these world travelers, much had not been
fair and many in their quest despaired.
Their torture grew in a hail of bullets, bombs, and bloody
lacerations and yet they persevered
staring ever forward across the narrow border divide.

The taste of freedom and equality, sought the hope
 their spirits desperately fought to obtain
in the nineteenth century.
In those eighteen hundred years, some achieved it,
while others died with it in plain sight.

What did these black bodies ever do
to deserve such punishment?
Being black was always under attack.
Yearning for fairness and impartiality
was a lie constantly soaking up
and polluting the air outside and in
when displayed on the face of antagonistic
sense of hatred.

Forever is time hiding from the light.
Forever is not rejecting the pain of a servile institution
that minute-by-minute shackles the neck,
back, and spirit of the screams,
freedom is made to accept by the whip.

The offer of fresh unsalted air would
and did arrive bit by bit,
year by year, mile after mile
when the mind of some posed an alternative solution
as old as time itself.
It was not new,
just due its course of actionable traction appearing

like an angel, like a maple leaf drifting
through the wind beautifying the landscape
in autumn.

In a time or moment such as this,
circumstances ascend the throne
to enlist one of humanities greatest gifts,
tolerance to difference
and the choice of engaging
what brotherhood understood.

These moral intuitions, known as cultural decency
was not buried but surfaced in a proposal
from one soul to another
from one stranger who chose to be a friend
and the other not to contend but accept an offer.

Goodness is a variant
like a Samaritan willing to extend his hand across
the divide, regardless of the mileage,
the acreage, on which he stood to close the gap.

Smiles and easy agreement
comprised of friendly discourse
severs unbridled negativity,
sponsoring useful, thoughtful- discovery
which is not foreboding.

Oh! Canada, you are truly my brother
And have been all the time....
(for W. G. the superior court Judge)

CONSTELLATION HARDIS MAJOR

Nine bluish-silver stars came together
to form the fantasy constellation: Hardis Major
whose identity placed them not too far
on this side of the newborn crystal nebula.

These stars each worked desperately hard
to mold a portion of their unique allotment.
The bar they faced was initially placed,
at what seemed beyond their immediate sight
though not their future reach,
for it to grace their mantle with golden satisfaction.

To achieve the dream, required a massive
front loaded self-esteem
to master and undo the pestilence
that often barred their perilous, mountain trails.

They needed extreme force from the beginning
of a challenging work-related career undertaking.
Life although given is seldom a guarantee of preserving.
It is a recurrence of continuity, struggle, toil,
and labor deeply applied
like a serious essay being written to gain
the mark of ultimate accomplishment.

Confidence and more
kept these heavenly bodies
from shutting the iron door,

where talent, skill, and hope lived in concert
with demonstrated will and determination to advance
into the light of satisfaction
against the odds of adversity's scraping claws.

Although many times,
the stars were clouded with distress
on a particular day.
They nevertheless buffed themselves clean,
redeeming their momentary resignation.

Life's demands opened their eyes
whenever the train's iron wheels screeched,
kicking up fire pins.
The nearness did not fold against itself
but removed the emotional debris
alongside the tracks which it could explain.

There was no cease and desist
in this life altering contest.
The winner would move on
and the loser restrained from living
beyond a sliver.

Against the blue-black heavenly carpet,
only the stars shone brightly
and dare not resist
but carved their location for others to monitor
their own progress.

Each one had her own speech well-rehearsed
and was clear in verse to make any change of course
should unsympathetic doubt seek to turn them inside out

like the crash of 29' that sent some colliding onto
the cement pavement below
regardless of their economy of effort.

Their unique story though inspiring is not the only one
applied to the role of accomplishment
but these nine stars are markers of profound morality
and principled behavior we all can call to mind
and feel within our hearts.

Dream- the-dream, fold it inward with persistence.
Place its value high above the bar
where stars reside in concert with the heavens.
There you will meet your history's success
in a scenic composition of beauty earned and deserved.

(Pamela, Stephania, Valerie, Agnes, Romania, Monika,
 Lilla, Denisa, Nina)

HER HEART

He was stolen; removed, taken all too soon
from earth's time and space.
Entombed, though not erased from her
wonderful heart's estate.

The discolored spot and pain remained
like a battered flag waiving, the inscription
of their motto, "love forever in the soul
shall never refrain from its domain".

He had come along
to greet her with his profound love
that was mighty and strong.

Together their golden rays
delighted one another's heartfelt wishes
given forth by the hand of the Lord
from His Holy Mountain on high.
There they knelt transfixed, humbled,
full of joy's magnificent message.

What they praised was ushered away
by a damaging sickness.
His body was recalled by a cancerous death
to a sad homecoming.

Life can be selfish.
Life can choose not to wait

and remove itself from their orchestrated plan,
stalling the hope that was grand.

In her pious heart, he was the eternal flame
not to be smothered, snuffed out, dampened.

The unseen venom, however struck first,
unwilling to quench the thirst, ignominy unleashed.

Its severity fell upon them like Satan's wrath
ripping apart his skin and bones
with its treasonous implants
determined to execute their future's quest,
that heretofore promised a blissful life
for them to honor.
Their hope was stamped, "closed for the season".

She was called upon to pose a solution,
to answer the unfortunate challenge,
one that for many may disfigure.

On her face, she however manifested
a calm non-visceral attitude.
Her posture demonstrated the strength of steel,
the iron will not to be deceived,
the striking, undaunted, fearlessness,
knights used when entering
the lists to do battle with the enemy.

Tomorrow would be built,
 with hope, and love once more,
regardless of the damage presented to their world.

Faith knows the valley and the harshness
that trots with each step
when we face dynamic losses
that serves to break down our foundations.

Over and over her fortitude was not fooled.
She raised her magical hammer
and pummeled the emotional enemy
seeking to slow her progress
and her children's destiny.

Sacrifice is the seed of growth.
Taking this avenue, she pulled
her family from the edge, the brink of defeat
with her astounding courage, majesty,
and moral endurance.

She is to be treasured, celebrated like the Alps,
the peaks of the Matterhorn, the western Rockies,
whose tremendous fortitude has withstood nature's tenacity.

She retained her natural beauty
refusing to crumble.
"These fortifications speak to the power
we truly have in our core's existence",
said her heart from their start"   ★P

BEFORE IT BEGINS

Before time, what was good
was only the air I could ingest
and breathe normally.

I proceeded from there still in a quandary
being catapulted through my mind
in a great agonizing struggle
with that which was left behind.
This unknown I carried with a frown.

I preferred a pouch filled with the riches
I felt it was my due.
Confusion surrounded my path
through this wilderness.
Life there lacked a conscious quality,
choosing to support extended devaluation instead.

Throughout that whirly world,
were many who failed to comprehend such values.
I was among those of lower conception.

I carried a sword that gourd the caliber of others.
Those glorified martyrs saw no evil,
Possessing only goodness which "the tree of life"
readily sponsored, and the world used to flourish.

Unfortunately, they were easily discarded,
manipulated, and denounced as spiritual bigots.
How could such a procession of harm
be allowed to continue festering?

Change needed to awaken, expanded, refreshed
that hatred be overcome and self-respect
spread across the land on which we sat.

When all seemed lost, I saw her today
and prayed no further sorrow would visit.

Her sweet, delectable countenance
drenched me with renewed revitalization
and a quest for life.
She was beautiful, in a long blue satin dress,
garnished by her greenish-brown eyes.

My belief in living spoke loudly, charmingly hopeful
in that immediate flash of illumination.
I renounced the realm of trifling disdain.
I felt the sun warming the nape of my neck.
My soul stood erect; my spirit warmed to the occasion.
I was freed from an enigmatic pestering control.

I discovered where I belonged
and thanked the Holy Spirit for His grace.
No longer would I be a wonderer
without a suitable portfolio,
nor pace for the meaning
of what it meant to be alive.

Her glorious comforting presence afforded
the blend of a new trend.

When help presided as a friend,
all could be right with the world
before it totally ends.   ★S

THE LAND OF ALL THINGS GOOD

Struggling on the precipice of failure,
The flush sound in her mellow voice
alerted me to my impending demise.

We were never all meant to be alike.
The autumn rainbow color leaves
informs and incites the truth
that constantly captivates.

Throughout a ragged life, conflict has raged,
determined to prove that single mindedness
is the correct attitude we must have to foster
unity of purpose.

Difference nevertheless suggests otherwise under the skin.
A salad is tastier with a variety of added ingredients
such as tomatoes, lettuce, cucumbers, croutons,
green peppers, a splash of spice
and honey mustard to stimulate the palate.

The canines are eager to see the particulars with enthusiasm
allowing them to reach the base of the stomach
with a certain degree of satisfaction.

When that promise is achieved, joy is not restrained
nor complains throughout the body and brain.

Thereafter, we can look at our surroundings without an
appeal.
We may wish to confirm the truth with distinction
being the prime directive gluttony thinks suitable
for forward advancement.

The choices which are made and stall
produce unruly behaviors that cast a distressing blow,
forcing disparity to bring about gross imbalances
to the community at large.

Subtraction is measured against the negative impact
and must search for its cowardly balance.

She ran from the road
and found bloody toads lining the gulley.
The shock bruised the inches of her skin.
They were no dizzy jubilation to ascertain
the rules of proper survival.

In her home, a better design,
 proved itself a great welcoming find
giving their world the answer
for multicultural, enlightened, peaceful, orchestration.

Most citizens chose to sit comfortably at different tables,
enjoying a pleasant meal like on Thanksgiving Day.
The Mauritius isle had held itself accountable to peace in its
time.   ★V

TRANSCENDING THE SCENE

Her discreet warmth, when delivered
stills the environment,
accentuating what is positive.

Her movements are calm and in full accord
with each demand made
by the multitude of strangers coming and going.

Though mostly reserved,
she displayed a silent charisma
in the face of harried requests, from overbearing,
self-indulgent, intractable, irritating creatures
who see themselves as very important.

No enigmatic distress is worth
such a high degree of alarm.
She supersedes these corrosive adults
entitled mindsets with her sublime professionalism.

Time and again she faced their rudeness
removing then with dispatch to the trash
using avowed discipline of service before self.

How she is to be recalled is rightly unknown.
What can be said however
is she kept her proper distance
with a wealth of royal cordiality.

Her pride never blocked
her respect for others
and a purpose which reflected
the role of a premier skillful worker
who never undermined devotion to duty. ★A

BETTER TIMES

Though we are of a different color pigmentation
which dresses our bones.
We can claim the bite from the similar
deadly savage scourge which attempted
to terminate the pounds of happiness it opposed.

The world has equal sides and stories to tell.
Unfortunately, these acid tales
are dramatically, disconcertingly woe full.

Their sadness shower tears like a cold waterfall
crashing upon the boulders below.
The unbearable, horrible, hurt latches unto the body
like an infamous virus seeking
to inflict its misery into the soul,
none of which is palatable.

East or west, the finest there is in a family may share
a distressing infamy to survive after losing
 a mother or father's once kind-hearted touch.

My life a long while ago
met the fate such as your do now.
To you I can only propose a measure
of secluded compatibility
to show sympathy
and a round of sound compassion.

The unease however which will persist
for days and years and not altogether stop
but subside in its own time
will allow you once again to glide.

Time ticks away,
beating against the frames of your fragile reality.

We are now gathered, first learning as strangers
on a friendly voyage of discovery.
Today we reached, crossing into the land
where defeat wishes to terminate the songs of life.

Tomorrow and perhaps years thereafter
You and I might come together,
and our forces once more smile,
that we may enter our hearts
from different sides of this still
uncharted bruising planet.   ★R

THE TIMES THAT WERE

There is a bold daring river
whose history stretches before AD.
The Calabrian age or 1.8 million years
to be more exact.
The Roman northern frontier border
was here in 454AD.

The Danube was formed at the confluence
of the Brigach and Breg as a spring
within the castle of Donaueschingen.

Today the Danube travels the length of 1770 miles
from the Black Forest Mountains
of Western Germany to the Black Sea.
It has stood the test of time
and played a vital role in Central and Eastern European
history.

The people who called home the miles it bordered
where often attacked and dominated by petty dictators,
whose mission was to exercise power and control
of their bodies and minds
like the previous Habsburg rulers
who cast their shadow on the Ottoman Empire.

The Russians took their turn later as well
but the land would not entirely succumb

to those who pilfered it with their aggression and arrogance.
They were only visitors moving through
in a frenetic confused dis-functional parade.
Their philosophy proved inconvenient to the masses
and wars broke out taking their toll on both human and
nature.

Hers are the genes of this unique history
bonded along the shorelines
of this lengthy emerald waterway.

Surviving and evolving is the quest of any living organism
that nature calls into play and not confine.
The quality of the life she hoped to achieve lies
 in the path of destiny's consultation
with trials and tribulations which must be overcome
and undone to make the run towards success.

She was molded from pure steel
and fourteen carat gold
deep within her soul.
She is the child of a resolute culture.

She had the strength of artful determination
and spiritual inspiration to travel forward
and assume the greatest heights
faith and belief in self musters.

There are times, moments,
when doubt may wish to occupy a place in one's
disposition.

She easily answered that alarm
instead of retreating into sadness
and tearful distress.

We are placed in places to act to cross bridges
that takes us to a broader awareness of the possibilities
we must follow to attain a brighter, larger scope
to evolve like "Ben-Hur" mounting
the chariot in the arena for the sake of improving his life.

The skills she possesses are like those the Danube extols.
They will make her surpass a million tears.
She was made to endure.
She was born to adorn the crown of saints
with red roses and deflect the uselessness
of intemperate malcontents.

This noble tidewater has been the home of fishermen,
sailors, drifters, and flotsam
who chose to make their way in a free and easy manner
while welcoming sunrises and sunsets.

The Danube has and will always be a good nurse
for the lonely heart, willing to plant a flower to mark its
glory.

PRINCESSES IN THE SKIES

Princesses in the skies
work hard to retain their glow.

Shining brightly is their invitation
being expressed from within
like a constant multicolored
Christmas tree show,
we can see from below the heavens
throughout the year.

Becoming dull or dim
is their soul flickering, withering.

The curse of time can rob them of their prime,
leaving them to shiver, rust,
and without mercy turn to dust.

Once they lived at the altar
of sterling stirrings that led the way
to harmony's unbridled occupation.

Mistrust in the spirit was never seen
but fought against, aspired, not to achieve.

They gracefully came into life
not merely to play
but rather to have their say

regarding the lushness
they could help convey
in support of "The Director's" heavenly plan.

Life for them was always a miracle
we strive to recognize.

Stars shared time and space.
Guided to the cosmos, earthly pioneers.
Patented astrological points of reference
which served those willing to risk life
in the pursuit of conquering miles
heretofore lost in wonder.

The princesses of such magnitude
transported beauty unmasked
which is meant to last
throughout the universe.   ★N

FIGHTING THE SEA OF LIFE

She is lithe, kind,
and gives the mind's eye
a try at joy
that satisfies the wounded heart.

Inside my head, I was glad
I overcame not being dead.
I found myself
and greeted the fractured script
whose marker read, "started and stopped
and that was that"

On the night in question, she removed herself.
Hell protruded in a wild, dynamic, spellbinding,
bewitching, bombshell.
I became altogether disorientated.

What there was of her to regain
 lay in a mound.
Painful revelations would not be desolate
nor vanish from the fray.
Dirt on the ground was a fair treaty
locked in my despair.

The celestial reflecting moons
which signaled distant suns
pitched their sympathetic concerns

like meteors roving across the night's sky
surmounting the yearnings to be cooled.

Crossing into the gladiator's pit
was a dangerous undertaking
for a simple misdemeanor about to occur.

Seeking the thrill resting, smoldering within lit feelings
 was like peering into the eyes
of a Cheshire Cat
who knew blood could easily be drawn
by a plain scrape from any attempted embrace.

The devil's revelry looked on.
She and I thought, "no harm no foul",
though what could be undone
after homespun spirits
sparked their way to having fun.

Mayhem gathered at their feet
to ambush the anticipated treat
they richly felt and needed to acquire
with excelling speed.

Reason would not clarify the impending deed.
Looking away cared only to play.

She discovered her first elusive burning passions.
He another conventional victory
at little cost for any loss.
The bait was cast but would it last?

Their fancy was primed and aimed at disturbing
fully, the workings inside their mental and physical
enclosures.
The fanfare neared the impatient salute with due respect.
The briefing transpired; their future was attired
and attested to their mindful expansion.

Hooked together like a sixty-pound giant tuna
racing with the fly in its jaws.
The battle for survival and happiness began.
Did they really comprehend the consequence, its sacrifice?

The fishing rod reeled off yards and yards of plastic line
from the reel under the might of the creature's defense.
The whirling sound of the reel continued to sing
with each tug the determined animal influenced.

The battle between man and beast persisted.
They were seriously locked into their self-serving
entertainment.

Towards the end and close to grand satisfaction,
no further words of wisdom did they utter.
Letting go was the preferred start.

Bitterness never marched from his mouth to her gleeful
tears.
They were seared.
Being mature, they maintained dignity and decorum.
Matched by formality and a classic flair.
They had only each other from which to depart.

In the captain's log, the entry read, "two hands left the sea after capturing a miracle opportunity to reward a candid affair".

Thereafter like bushels of rain,
Not even tomorrow could explain the outcome
to their brains.

BEYOND THE PRESENT

It was a nice pristine day
and I went for a stroll
to amplify my stay from
west of the Black Sea.

I prayed from my kneecaps,
wishing and hoping our world together
would expand rather than contract and uncross.

The life we had unearthed
was grounded in apparent fact
but began deepening the unchecked possibility
of a potent, agreeable, hospitality.

Two flexible souls sought to unify
their eternal spirits waded into the mist
of an amicable, tantalizing search for holy benefits.

They were prepared to tackle the distance,
the probable challenges, and outright pain
which would force itself to worsen
any aspect of their collaboration.

Miles like raging tides rose and fell,
though no screaming was heard between them
and goodwill continued to prosper and flow.

Tentacles like those of a quid
extended themselves like protection
guarding their courtesy from dissatisfaction.

The conveyances furnished,
stipulated that payment for any misdeed
must be collected post-haste.

Gratitude for their coincidence however
stepped forward without a moment's pause
onto the pedestal of kindly jubilation.

The love inside them was very strong
and intent on, should a seismic, earth-shattering howl
bend the branches, from a twenty story
nearby evergreens occur,
they would remain committed to their integrity.

Sleep could not deposit its ease upon their roaring pyre.
They saw the grip of life conspire to maintain its ire
and befriend the frank honesty which accompanies
the result of ultimate time together.

The aggressive march was that of the Legion
bent on solving the truth of their commitment.
From her to him the curse did not waver.

The endeavor would not crack
nor check itself at the door.
Hope appointed itself the greater good,
Something they both uniformly readily understood.

Their light impeded the rule of darkness.

Friendship proved a more lasting, suitable,
opportune occasion to honor
at the behest of their request,
"From any shore they wished to beseech" …

THE SCENIC ROAD TO TRAVEL

My words are the arrows and shields
that stem the assault of others
who for their own sake,
 seek to puncture my spiritual soul
while raking the goodness
buried in my heart's constitution.

With each abstract thought,
I fueled challenging emotions,
built a moat to protect
the royal castle in which I reside,
from Mongol hordes lurking in the night.

These foul, misguided sores,
continued their daily attacks
against the storehouse of my sentiments.
They snuck around to any unprotected entry
and lit their fires.

I needed to guard against their salted minds,
that attempted to scale the walls
in hopes of breaching the fortress ramparts
with axe and pitchforks.

Their desire was to spill buckets of blood
from the body's flesh.

The challenge weighed heavily
upon the crown above my head.

I had to cover each angle at risk
and repulse their feeble endeavor
with a stern disregard.

I fired a wave of deadly verbiage
that quelled the beastly onslaught
used by the mean-spirited evil doers.

The bombshell drew a rise
like the sea overpowering the shore,
raking the sand which the land adored.

Words can weaken; they can also steal
the good imbedded in the soul
or heal any deficit revealed.

These tools I pack on my back in bunches
to ward off unseen or heard surprises.

Words help us to govern the borders of our existence
with precise effort and splendid artistic resilience.
It is also true for what we mean to do.

⸻⟁⟁⟁⸻

A LITTLE DREAM

The quietness of her allure
bid me explore with extreme deportment
and extended energy which her intense attraction
lurking beneath the sighing our goals couldn't control.

Her long but strong fingers kept the inquiry alive,
dive after dive while I canvassed the altar along
her mountain peaks and valleys.

Superb views were also seen on the slopes and crevices
that rimmed the parameters of her stellar rareness
where the air was thin and battled parts of the body within.

Love and conflict were locked in torrid transactions
with delight, suffocating their neutral understanding.

For eons scenic expanses of marvels such as Everest,
K2 or Cho Oyu in the Himalayas was accepted
as the privilege for the minds of the fortunate.

Love and desire as we know is blinded in the heat of passion
instead of compassion.
Both electrical cords funnel through
a complex array of self-discovery
based on risk, individualism,
and the lure of diversity's magnetic appeal.

The taste unleashes miraculous waters
which The Spirit defines as positive alliances.

In many parts of the planet
interest in travel has played a key role
in weaving togetherness out of multiculturalism.

Differences have been the bedrock for those
who wished to sponsor a new matrix for evolution.
Oneness has profited the few at the expense of the many
like retarding the expansion of the galaxy,
keeping the stars as a definition of solely our own property.

The world is here to adore, tour, seek,
 and condone for its own beauty,
like the face that had me embrace its body's howling
and miraculous richness in a single word.

Openness is the key that leads to our harvest
in the spring, summer, autumn,
and beside the crackling fires at Christmas time
when treasures are hung
and the heart sings tiding's of joy.

KALOCSA (LILLA)

The straw of life is formed
by the noble order of the "protectors",
who take the spiritual oath of sacrifice for those
who cannot function alone by themselves
but must be defended, provided for.

Through her youthful years,
she raised her shield against
misfortune's attacks,
by waging an intense battle to succeed,
regardless of the cost
to her own personal loss of love or happiness.

Her path encountered rocky, uneven, avenues
filled with adversity that she managed
to thoughtfully blocked
and thereby overpowered
with emotional strength and care.

She postponed and set aside her own dreams of success,
of expanding her geographic borders,
tasting the world's sophisticated offerings.

Patience was her willing aristocratic cause
that did not blur her resolve
and commitment to the oath she took
to sacrifice and support.
Her perseverance pointed its head high.

Her life though filled with fascination,
kept pondering,
chasing time's admission to the growth,
she would not let be subject to failure.

A positive mindset made her not fall behind
nor below the rock of aging.
She summoned and mounted spirited attacks often,
against opportunities she had to allow fall-away, into the
ground.

Her vision was for the just cause,
she swore to rightfully assist,
rather than resist and desolve into emotional distress.

Faith in her soul and spirit
proposed to her,
the river on which to sail onward.
Her courage assailed the turbulence
whirling from the east and west.
She navigated their swift currents,
forded sandbars, and minor waterfalls,
that demonstrated themselves in common display.

Obstacles were foolish designs for the uncommitted mind.
Hers did not subscribe to such meanderings.
She was ever steadfast, and goal directed.

Beauty as ever, followed upon her countenance
as a true compatriot and place to take its stand.
Lilla is honorable to the needs of her family
and the responsibility of being the first born.

Her unwrinkled, polished facial features accentuated the
positive,
while erasing any gloomy distortions,
wishing to present themselves
on her smooth friendly cheekbones or forehead.

She is the pure representative child
of her cultural genes.   ★L

SCENIC NIGHT'S BASH

The night fashioned its robe
with an unusual array of bright twinkling,
sparkling crystal orbs.
The musical crescendos added
to its parade of flashing lights.

The friskiness on the dance floor
alerted the dancers to commit
their bodies to the bouncing beat
resonating off the scenic walls.

The stage stood ready to comment
with vocal, salivating vigor.

Those mashing their heels
on the hard linoleum floor
slid easily from side to side
compiling an energizing display of creative memories.

Those with their waning skills
 returned for one more run at fame
with memorable "twisting" dance numbers.

The crowd in a mesmerizing chant,
release themselves like an apparition applying
its own very pleasing appetite.

The floor was scuffed inch by inch
with the twirling, stomping, and scaring

initiated by uncompromising music,
calling upon their twilight spirits.

Among the throng and sweating horde,
her deep shiny raven hair and intense blue eyes
took me to the farthest reaches of the heavenly skies.

Our dance styles were a mixture of east and west,
Motown of the sixties
and Eastern European of the twenty first century.

She performed like a bold meteor cruising through God's
splendid universe. Joy filled her unique form as we twirled
and spun around.
Our energies paved the way to unadulterated happiness.

The impact she made,
restored the fabled legends surrounding Greek and Roman
goddesses
whose power in their beauty ruled man's geography and
impending destiny.
Their captivating presence and aura drove those athletes to
their knees.

One look into those astounding magnetic optics
would wipe clean their souls, from a fragile body.
She could reach down and savor their wilting heart.

From the start
I was helpless to conclude her summons within my chest.

More was at a loss to finish or engage further
her intense mercurial gaze
which announces the arrival of the Lord's angel.

I felt a perfect brush against my arms, touch my fingers,
bonding us to address the miracle music
that melted our fragile forthcoming.

The pure energy in her celestial composition
spoke the language of incandescent radiation.
Our meeting and greeting comported themselves
with relief and belief in the heart's beholding.

Another day with her spirit close at hand
would lend profound possibility
to the wishes I hope to acknowledge.

Light years or possibly one could not maintain
the pain goodbye would have to address.

Her mouth uttered reality.
I turned from yearning.
Possibility burned the fever later
from what I was to learn.

Joy's eagerness lent itself to the melody
and circumstances born by happenstance.
Forgiveness waited down the road
carrying a heavy load.
The afterlife is still answerable
to the potency of agape's next visit…

THE VESSEL OR YOU

In five days, I'll need not pretend
nor defend the distance,
I wish to apprehend.
Whenever I see your sapphire eyes
and demure lips
that attempt to provoke in me their wish to visit.

I rear up inside and must decide
should I restrain the quake
that suddenly rumbles?

The magnetic pull squeezes my breast,
depressing the air from its lungs
like a parasite sucking bits of life
the host previously secured.

Are you what or how you wish would assure
a fruitful experience,
a lasting explosion of fantastic proportions?
Are you the potent, effectual, lively one
that caused time to cease its charge,
by devouring rhythmic rhymes
in their ongoing promotion?

The mind can morph into "sweet soul music"
at the request of sixties memories,
when one body leaned against the other

in the same place, alerting rapid emotions,
emboldening, exploding feelings,
to cry havoc and cling their hips.

Those were the days and more so, the heated night,
when good understood its tasteful accentuations
and vivid collaborations.

Their spiritual prayers conveyed honesty
and to them a sign appeared
which life illusions aborted.

The bend in the river posed no recall.
They engaged the fray
and a truce was assigned.

I cheered for the valiant assimilation
knowing that time between us would end,
whether she was to be a stranger
or a meaningful friend.

One without redress or a slow confession
which extended the minutes
we had to offer the shallow tides
above the slippery sand…

BOAT, THANK YOU

The unhurried greenish waters
executed its own flowing style
in the sometimes calm, rippling,
wavy currents moving beneath the hull of the boat.

Throughout her royal existence, Scenic has touched
the borders of many different countries
along the Danube's 1770 miles.

Exalted music and waltzes
have paid tribute to her journey.
She has hosted numerous
individuals from countries as distant as Australia,
the USA, Canada, UK, and others.

All these passengers had only good things to say
about the services received and the variety of history
imparted along the way.

The onboard entertainment proved an unexpected delight
from classical instrumentalist to vocal pop
and ballet and cultural dancing.

Our pallet was also unanimously sated.
When sleep landed, we closed our eyes and drifted quickly
into the arms of dreams.
Little if any rocking movement was perceived
before sunrise appeared as a surprise for the hours that passed.

Castles upon castle drifted by along the hillsides
displaying their history going back through centuries of
change.

Fulfillment existed within this example of Noah's arc
and like the contacts made, memories will sustain us
until we seek again another collusion with time
aboard a vessel such as this,
and the cities and countries left to visit.

Being instructed by their position in Eastern European history
closed the book on the miles floated.

Until then I can say goodbye
to all who saw or think of me as I them, a friend.

Though it may seem unofficial, their service's value was of
great importance
to the outcome of the passenger's journey.
Gratitude is often more than simply thanks.
The mark it leaves is a meaningful treasure conceived
and the joy the mind holds long after years terminate.

Thank you to the organizing specialist as well
who arranged the outstanding activities,
food delicacies, administrative flows of the passengers.
Viva the captain, who took us and safely brought us back to
land!

LONG SEASONS TO REMEMBER

Give me justice or donate my soul to a hole
where there is no light to behold.

Justice had left town weeks and years before.
It was lost, eroded, corroded, demoted by lies
and the beliefs of cowards
to delicate not to conform
and perform right-minded legal decisions.

They were instead willing to destroy
the blood of humanity's pride.

I am not just a black man
on the road attempting to orchestrate
life's promised hold.
I am the minutes suffering with strife
that is holding the knife at my throat.

The brutal illogical device
has through the assent of time
won its case without disgrace
and applauded each conclusion demonstrated.

Laughter during the turmoil
slipped into a corner to count its reverie
like death's hallows dropping their autumn leaves
on the dirt mound in the distant, tired,
back lot, bought and sold.

Living above this earth,
once planted with positive memories
that worked to contribute its validity, vitality,
 is now confused by hatred and misdirection.

The hours became tired of the perspective
established to harbor clandestine denials
and unwholesome, improper adjudications.

The hurting minds and spirit of the decent folk
were punished for existing and wishing to grow.
Hope and respect were not tolerated
in the heart of the devil's preconceptions.

Black must be removed,
constantly demoted, to inferior status
to perform mindless tasks.

Jail awaited its summons
for a life judged by a lack of objectivity.
Bias and prejudice knew their role
and performed it with total indifference,
to the saints.

I am a black constantly seeking fair play
most often delayed, robbed of his stalwart stance.
Anger remained for him to get along
before crossing the road into oblivion.
The aging electrical juice rang its bell.

Hell did not refuse to tell his story
of blight between light and eternal darkness
which compelled blacks to deliver
their souls once more
to this seemingly shallow hopeless life.

We blacks were told often by evil
to request mercy but it did not reply.
Mercy only wanted us to comply
with sacrifice and blood.

Concerned with why was totally unnecessary.
The bronze scales of justice had long been broken.
Stained by the gift of bigotry
and ruthless disharmony.

The balance in the fight was fixed
since its inception, with collusion,
which couldn't resist the delusion
branded as equality for all.

This falsehood was easily removed
and repeatedly used and reused
as a token belief in God.
who lived in the neighborhood
that wasn't good enough for coloreds
and other distinctive brothers and sisters.

THE BROWN FEDORA

1989, the brown fedora sat in his closet
gathering dust.
He had worn it occasionally.
Oil from his skin painted the inside rim.

He had owned that hat since 1983.
It lay in a dark room unused for most of its life.

I took it back with me after the funeral,
preferring to have the memory,
rather than consigning it to The Goodwill Store.

Hats of that style
reflect a specific style in history,
when men dressed elegantly
whenever Saturday night came around.

From head to toe, they presented experience
and maturity.
When shoes were worn, they were impeccably shined.
The trousers were creased sharply.
White handkerchiefs adorned left coat pockets,
to be an assistant when needed.

Black sox consistently matched the attire.
The hat, however, was tilted to one angle or the other
to demonstrate a certain attitude of strength or danger.

The mustache was specific, short,
 but not hanging beyond the corners or over the lips.
Each of his fingernails were cleanly cut
 and sometimes manicured.

A haircut was also required to accentuate orderliness.
If the gentleman had a beard, it too was orchestrated
to display neatness.

This presentation fit my dad in life and in death.
The fedora did well that day.
Two for the price of one.

I tried to quiet my pain and not complain.
The hat, however, said he would remain,
confronting me with its stain.

It lives on still crowding my heart
with a certain amount of anger for the loss.

The brown fedora is a dire conspirator
to the consequence living promotes.

THE WISH

Girl, I wish you were the woman
I had cause to understand
and not withstand.

If you were, we could then discover the means
to transport ourselves together to the end of time,
without cease being inspired.

"Take my hand", he said.
Allow my mind to rest next to your warm head
and divine its sanctuary where I'll ultimately sleep
without retreating after confessing all you mean to me.

What you'll find, could align
both quadrants in the known universe
and sprinkle their stars generously
across heavenly terrain.

Soon their diminishing travels halted.
The port of call looked toward a new blessing
but was disqualified due to extenuating circumstances.
The mire gave into sorrowful contemplation.

Love is mostly the ache
governing an insipid spiritless vacuum
that grips and rips at the soul,
asking to be forgiven for purposes still unclear.

What we choose, need not prevail
especially when its means are curtailed
from the image time chose to resist
and eventually deny.

Girl you are beyond good and have circulated within
the inches of my galaxy taking me to the home
of a conclusive revelation where the voice of Eden is ideal.

Fate there long awaited your entry
through its front gate, to honor inspiration
like the call of joy quieting the unsung consternation.

I have reached back into time's incantation,
discovering the precious, splendid, gem
only you carried and could ever satisfy my vault.
The red glow beats as it testifies
between knowledge and its significant transmission.

THE VOYAGE

Am I a fool for you?
Tell me the truth
or let me cease being confused.

My heart is at a loss,
bewildered by strained feelings.
The conflict continues to cloud the room
wherein I stand.

Remaining firm is like drowning beneath the seas.
She shipped me away for the sharks
to tease me like a tormented display.

Each three-inch incisor, she used,
 cut me with a spirited acclamation.
I was dragged and deeply torn apart
to be disposed under saline waves.

Nothing about her exposure was just.
Watching the disappearing act
only punctuated my remains.

Her willful love was our fake filled debate.
Today, yesterday, and tomorrow,
which held the passage through weighted sorrow,
begged for nothing to further enhance
the degree of insanity that filled our wounds.

Unbelievable as she was,
nothing I felt could be spared its dissolution.
The rule of mishap was sharp
and played its harp, precisely.

Under the strain, Love was given a final chance
to include itself in the big dance.
Win and continue, lose, and retire.

The heart's position was at stake.
Her quiet desire fashioned a smile.
I didn't idle
but found myself, not again being a fool
who chose rather to stay in school
and learn not to refuse,
 beauty's thunder.

FEELINGS WE CONVEY

Where do your feelings evolve?
Where do you thrive?
How much do you give from inside?
Do you hide?

What feelings does it take to keep you alive?
What specific feelings motivate you?
What kind of feelings can you easily translate?
How much can feelings stimulate?
How will feelings survive a particular state of mind?

What feelings are you inclined to absorb?
What type of feelings make you blue?
What feeling tells you, you are true.?
How do your feelings know what to do?
Do your feelings lie?
Do they help you to try?

Do they realize the truth of your desires?
Do your feelings contrive to keep you alive?
When will your feelings cease to make you persist?
When do your feelings know the way of understanding?
Why do your feelings gravitate to the dark side?
When do your feelings become selfish?
When do you not try to resist?
What makes your feelings rise to the height of a seismic
  wave?

Why did your feelings choose to deliberate?
Why did you seek or wish to translate their desires?
Why did you have to feel anything?
Did your scream release the feelings you would like to
deliver?

VOICE OF A CHAMPION

Goodness will always remain
near and dear to us.
Once in a great while a voice such as hers surfaces
and helps us refocus our priorities.

Time had this opportunity.
Took it, and we thrived for a short
though meaningful period.

Her presence brightened the feeling
of the heavens sitting above our heads.
Compassion inspired new deliberations.
Hope stood up and called for awareness
rooted in the need for change and relevancy.

She came, saw, and explained, the benefits of collaboration.
The insightful message, instigated momentum in the minds
of those who had waited and waited to confirm the vision
of support and truth.

We were all in the position to gain
from what brotherhood and a community uplifting response
needed to explain.

Bettering the environment
through positive, enlightening messaging,
served to open new passageways
for self-improvement across a broader border,

that heretofore was minimal,
somewhat indifferent to equal sharing.

"Certain neighborhoods" felt they were left behind.
They cried out to be sustained.
The silence received was deafening.

Keeping faith, they tried to cope the best they could.
Though they were less than appreciably understood.

The appearance of the locality
 desperately required change
but it was left dripping to the ground
until a clear informing tone rose
and kept enlightening those
who could and should address the difficulty
within and outside the district,
by upgrading the advancement indicated.

Enhancement and refinement
finally made their way into the forefront
of rectification in the quality of living spaces
around the town/city of Spokane.

Advocacy and goodwill stood side by side
like the great spirit and vision of "Harriet"
facing up to the forces of past debilitations.

The determined spirit in her alternatives spread,
capturing the thoughts and hearts,
of the young, old, and in-between.

Black Lens News was born
and engaged, informed, the public at large.
This was the thunder, the lightning
darkness had need to deliver.

The locality's eyes were opened,
and forward movement tested.

Joy seemed to feel, the previous concern
for the awakening
of what was possible, doable,
and doable was change
and ultimate improvements
for its many surroundings.

Sandy's gift was an opportunity for others
that they may continue to dream and prosper
in whatever area of the city, they call home.

Though she is gone physically.
We shall never be alone without her.
Her eyes are still focused on the prize.

ACKNOWLEDGMENTS

Front cover: picture of Mt. Rainier
Back cover: picture of Mt. Rainier with poet in the foreground.

Front cover, picture taken by the poet, SJP
Back cover: Mt. Rainier with poet in the foreground, picture taken by Halle K-P

Made in United States
Troutdale, OR
03/07/2024